Pudd...

Marilyn Foote

TATE PUBLISHING & Enterprises

Published by Tate Publishing & Enterprises, LLC
127 E. Trade Center Terrace | Mustang, Oklahoma 73064 USA
1.888.361.9473 | www.tatepublishing.com

Tate Publishing is committed to excellence in the publishing industry. The company reflects the philosophy established by the founders, based on Psalm 68:11,
"The Lord gave the word and great was the company of those who published it."

Published in the United States of America

ISBN: 978-1-60462-883-8
1. Kids, Ages 6-10   2. Juvenile Fiction: Religious: Christian
08.02.20

I would like to dedicate my first book, *Puddinhead*, to my family. We are the children of Lonnie Charles and Mary Ellen Foote. We are seven girls; the youngest and eighth member is my brother. Without them, I would not have had playmates with whom to enact all our pretend play.

I thank God for blessing me with the skill to write and a vivid imagination. He is my guiding light in all things. I would also like to thank my Christian family from church, work, and writer's groups that have constantly prayed, encouraged, and supported me.

To Catherine!
God Bless You!
M. Foote

TABLE OF CONTENTS

The Foote family living room was glowing as the summer evening sun started to set. The large front window had a golden haze, and the seasonal breeze flipped the drapes lightly from the opened front door. Dinner was over; the table had bare evidence that a large family of seven had just completed their meal. The bright kitchen light beamed through the narrow hallway into the living room, and the clanging sounds of dishes meant that the two older sisters, Leah and Eve, were washing them.

Slowly and carefully Miriam, in search of her favorite quiet place, tip-toed into the house—peering at the hallway, making sure that her footsteps were quieter than the kitchen chatter. She did not want her two older sisters to know she was there. Miriam spied the large red chair in the corner. This was daddy's favorite chair that she loved to sit in as well. Climbing into the chair, Miriam could feel immediately the soft, fuzzy comfort of the high back. Miriam snuggled her head and posterior into the chair as if her little body had made a permanent impression there from frequent usage. The chair's warmth soothed her limbs, her legs dangled, she settled down, and Miriam closed her eyes. This was a frequent past-time for Miriam from the moment she could climb up onto the chair, since she was a baby, five years ago.

The peaceful thoughts floating through her mind took on a tranquil rhythm. Miriam responded by gently rocking back and forth. She listened to everything going on around her and replayed her whole day: the kitchen din; Leah, the eldest sister, singing softly with radio music; cars passing; locusts buzzing; the neighbor Mrs. Ford calling Abby, her best friend, to come home; her older sister Zirah playing upstairs; and a baby crying. That must be Emmanuel, Jr., the youngest. Mom was giving him a bath. Miriam smiled to herself because the day was restful, and she was very thankful for all the fun moments. Silently, she thanked God for such a good day. Miriam had learned in Sunday School that this was one way to start talking to Him. It made her happy to tell God things. She made sure that each time she sat in her chair, she prayed to Him.

Miriam's peace was suddenly shattered as voices became a little louder. Leah spoke to Eve, "I can tell that Miriam is in the living room."

Leah called out, "Is that you, Miriam? Come here right now!"

The living room was very dim, and shadows began to move across the wall.

Miriam squirmed into the chair trying to hide in its folds. She thought, squeezing her eyes shut, "*Oh, please don't come in here to find me!*"

Then, Eve teasingly said, "Miriam, I know you are in there rocking your brains out. Don't try to hide." Leah and Eve giggled a bit.

Leah added, "You know, if you continue to rock like that, your brain is going to turn into pudding. We are going to call you 'Puddinhead'!"

Leah and Eve started chanting, "Puddinhead, Puddinhead!"

Zirah, who heard the teasing, came downstairs and joined them in their chant.

Mom came down with Emmanuel, Jr., and quieted everyone. At the same time, Miriam timidly walked into the kitchen, frowning because the lighting was different between the living room and the kitchen. Mom asked what all the fuss was about. Everyone tried to talk at the same time, collectively exclaiming, "Miriam's brain is turning into pudding!"

Miriam just buried her head into her mom's lap. Seeing that Miriam was the target for the joking, Mom reminded everyone that they had all wanted a rocking chair to rock in last Christmas for a present. That settled everyone down. She decided to take Miriam upstairs. Mom told Leah and Eve to finish their work. Before she took Zirah and Miriam upstairs to give them their baths, Mom put Emmanuel, Jr., down to sleep.

Sitting in the bathtub was relaxing and warm. Miriam thought of a big pool to dive in and swim around. She loved the water, and she always dreamed of oceans and swimming pools. The cool, blue water preoccupied Miriam's mind all the time. She put her hands together over her head pretending she was going to jump. Mom watched as she washed Zirah's back.

"Miriam," she said, "When you rock in the red chair, tell me, what is going on in your head?" Zirah turned to speak, but Mom put a finger on her lips that silenced her.

Miriam squinted and turned her head from left to right. Then she added a grimace and pulled in her lips. She noticed that both Mom and Zirah were waiting for her to answer. She let out a small puff of air.

"Mom, I am thinking about thinking sometimes. I think about everything around me. I hear many things, and I need to think about them again. Sometimes I can hear whispers of someone talking to me."

Mom asked, "What is it saying?"

Miriam paused in deep thought. Mom was ready to ask another question when she finally answered. "Mom, I believe that God tells me things about what I should do and how to be good." Miriam closed her eyes and bowed her head, thinking her Mom might be upset with her.

But Mom was amazed at her daughter's answer; she would be just six years old in November, and that was three months away.

Zirah jumped into the conversation. "That is what Leah teaches us when we play school. She tells us that we have to think and listen because God wants to talk to us."

Mom took a double take and looked at both of her daughters. Zirah was only seven and half. Mom now comprehended that her daughters were really paying more attention than expected in Sunday school, and Leah was helping them to understand.

"So while you are rocking, you are talking to God?" Mom asked. Miriam misunderstood Mom's stare, thinking that Mom was not happy. Mom seemed to have a worried look on her face, and that scared her.

Then, Mom smiled and caressed Miriam's head in a loving way. Mom asked, "I can see that your quiet time on the red chair is very special for you. Do both of you like going to church and Sunday School with Grannie? Would you like to show little Emmanuel Jr. your lessons from church? We can all sit together after dinner on Sunday."

M iriam spoke quickly. "Yes, Yes, Yes. That would be a lot of fun!" Then, changing the subject, Miriam said with excitement, "I like to eat pudding too."

Zirah started laughing. "I like pudding too. Can we have some pudding?" Mom laughed and said she would make some for their snack. She gave each of them a small hug.

Miriam exclaimed that she could eat 100 bowls of pudding filling her head so full that she could really be called a Puddinhead.

Zirah chimed in,

"Puddinhead! Puddinhead! Puddinhead! Puddinhead!"

Miriam bounced in the tub to the rhythm of the name.

Leah and Eve joined the clamor as they ran up the stairs. Zirah asked Miriam, "Do you like this nickname?"

Miriam screamed, "Yeah!"

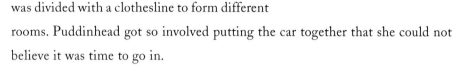

Puddinhead's day was very busy playing outside with her sisters Zirah, Leah, and Eve. She almost forgot to seek her beloved spot. The time just seemed to fly by. The girls built a makeshift house in the backyard. They used a large refrigerator box as their car. The yard was divided with a clothesline to form different rooms. Puddinhead got so involved putting the car together that she could not believe it was time to go in.

Leah, the oldest, was starting to read Puddinhead's moods. She sensed that Puddinhead was getting distracted and did not want to play anymore. Ever since Miriam agreed to be called Puddinhead, because she rocked in the large red chair, Leah felt she should be responsible to always know where she was. Leah was starting to enjoy talking to Puddinhead. She became an excellent tutor for such a willing student to teach her everything from reading and writing, to anything she learned at church.

Sure enough, Puddinhead asked to go inside to go to the bathroom. Leah followed discreetly behind her and watched as Puddinhead searched out her desired place to rest. Puddinhead climbed into the big red chair in the living room, savoring the awaited moment when she could relax and rock. The comfort of sitting alone while she gently swayed back and forth was the peaceful time that Puddinhead needed. Leah noted that Puddinhead was singing quietly as she rocked. Leah knew the song, but the words were not so clear the way Puddinhead was saying them. Then the melody came to her. Puddinhead was trying to sing "Jesus Loves Me."

Leah walked carefully up to Puddinhead and almost startled her. Puddinhead sounded a little like she wanted to cry, but quickly calmed down.

"Puddinhead," said Leah. "I know that song too. Do you want me to teach it to you?" Puddinhead accepted the interruption and made a space for Leah to sit next to her.

Leah's voice was so lovely while she sang,

Jesus loves me this I know.
For the Bible tells me so.

Puddinhead followed, listening to all the words. Shortly afterwards, Puddinhead got all of them and begged Leah to let her try singing the song all by herself. Leah was happy that she could be part of Puddinhead's quiet time and felt more encouraged to talk to her.

Leah shyly asked a question she had wanted to ask Puddinhead for a very long time. She began slowly. "Puddinhead, you have been sitting in this chair since you were a baby?"

Puddinhead thought for a moment, and she just nodded her head.

"What are you thinking about?" Leah spoke fast, so the question could be answered quickly.

Puddinhead closed her eyes as though she was figuring what would be a good response. Then she said, "Everything I see, hear, and learn. I just think about them." Puddinhead continued, "Like this song I learned at church. I can sing it, and now I am looking for God to smile on me. For as long as I can remember, that is what I do while I rock."

Puddinhead loved to talk with Leah. She was the only sister that took the time to talk to her about her quiet time and she started to understand her more.

Leah thought about what Puddinhead just said. "You are not even six years old yet. Do you really listen to the pastor at church? Most of the time your head is laying on Grannie's lap while you sleep."

Puddinhead looked Leah right in the eye and said with a little emotion, "I am listening to God talk to me!"

Leah raised her hand to try to calm Puddinhead down. She assured Puddinhead that she believed her.

Puddinhead added that she knew the song about Jesus loving all the children was true because she had asked Him. He said that He loves all the babies that cry all the time and even mean old Mark who lives down the street.

eah giggled and hugged Puddinhead. Leah added, "God is really good if He could love Mark as well!"

Puddinhead thought for a minute. "Grannie said that I have to pray for everyone, even if I do not like them. Is that true?"

Leah saw something in Puddinhead that was different and nice. Leah felt her little sister's eager stare as she tried to find the right words to answer her question. Leah could tell that Puddinhead, even though she was very young, was showing that she really believed in God.

Ugly Shoes

It was 6:00 a.m. and the girls, Puddinhead and Zirah, got up early to watch and listen to the morning sunrise. They were sitting on the porch, still in their pajamas and barefoot. "It feels like fall is coming early," remarked Zirah to Puddinhead. "I can see the clouds are too big for summer clouds, and the shade is starting to feel cool." Puddinhead always listened to her sister Zirah because Zirah had so much to tell her.

Puddinhead then looked up into the sky and tried to see what Zirah was talking about. "But you said last night that the weather was going to be hot today, and maybe Daddy could take us swimming," Puddinhead remarked.

Zirah put her finger on her cheek as she was thinking of the right thing to say. "Puddinhead," Zirah responded very seriously. "You are not old enough to really see what I am saying. When you get to see more August times, you can understand how it could be a little cool and then hot later on."

Puddinhead did not like that Zirah said she could not understand. She stood up and put her hands on her hips ready to argue. Zirah saw and knew what Puddinhead was about to do, so she said quickly, "All right already, I will try to explain!"

The squeaking of their neighbor's screen door caught the girls' attention. It was Mr. Ford, Abby's father, leaving to go to work. Zirah and Puddinhead jumped up and ran down the street to see if Abby could come out and play.

Mr. Ford said, "You two are early birds. Abby is still sleeping. You will have to wait for a couple more hours."

The girls started to return to their house, but Puddinhead liked the way the warm ground felt on her feet so much that she just started walking slowly down the street and looking up in the sky. Her arms were stretched out to the sides as if she needed them to help balance herself. She walked, delicately turning her wrists and moving her fingers. Zirah, already back at home, sat on the ground watching her sister. When Puddinhead got to the big tree about four houses down, she turned around with excitement shown on her face.

Puddinhead called from down the street to Zirah, "When I walk, the sun is warm on my face. But when there is a slight breeze, I don't feel the same warmth. It feels cooler. The air seems cooler in temperature. That's it! Isn't it?" Puddinhead shrieked! Puddinhead leaped several times because of her discovery and started to run back to her house. "Zirah, Zirah, I understand now!" she yelled.

Just before Puddinhead got to the front of her house, she stopped abruptly and cried out. Zirah thought that she stepped on something and came to help her sister. After a close examination, Zirah could find nothing wrong with Puddinhead's feet. Puddinhead was really crying now and exclaimed that her feet were hurting a lot. They both went into the house to show their Mom.

Mom said that they would have to wait until their daddy got home. The rest of the day was terrible for Puddinhead. Her feet just kept on aching. This time Puddinhead sat in the red chair, trying to console herself while she was dreaming about all the fun she could have had that day. She thought of running super fast, jumping the highest she could ever jump, and feeling the wind on her face. Then, she would have danced on her toes and nothing could have stopped her. This kept her mind off all the pain.

It wasn't the first time Puddinhead's feet had done this. Many times before, Puddinhead would be in the middle of playing, running, jumping, and simply walking. Then her feet would ache so badly that she'd sit down for the whole day, sobbing buckets of tears.

When Daddy came in from work early, he took Puddinhead to a foot doctor. This doctor said that Puddinhead had to wear a special pair of shoes with good arch supports. The doctor tried to speak very simply to her "You have what we call flat feet. This is when you have no arch."

"No arch? Flat feet! What is an arch, sir?" Puddinhead spoke in a panic to the doctor. The doctor explained to Puddinhead and her daddy how her feet had a special shape and how the muscles needed more support.

After the doctor's visit, they went to a shoe store. Tons of different and pretty shoes were there, and Puddinhead got excited. She gazed at several in the corner, but the shoe-store man kept on motioning her over to a table that had shoes that looked unattractive. She scooped up a few white and pink shoes and came over to Dad to ask him if she could try on these. He re-explained that the doctor wanted her to wear a special shoe to help with the flat feet. Puddinhead turned up her nose at the sight of the shoes the store owner showed her. They were called high-tops, and they tied-up. They were brown, not pink. She looked at her daddy with an expression saying, "I do not want them."

Daddy saw the face but responded, "You have to get these."

Puddinhead pouted, but she still got a pair of ugly, *ugly* shoes. Daddy had to talk with Puddinhead very sternly before they left the store.

"Puddinhead," he said, "I know you don't like your new shoes. You have to wear them anyway. Your feet are too flat, and that is why they hurt."

Puddinhead sulked all the way home as she looked at her feet. She whined, "They look bigger than normal. They weigh a ton. I cannot keep my feet straight. Everyone will laugh at me. I look like a clown. How can I possibly run fast wearing these shoes? These are ugly, ugly, *ugly* shoes!"

Daddy helped Puddinhead out of the car, but she did not move from its side. He walked up to the house and turned to see her still standing there.

"Come on, Puddinhead," said Daddy. "Think of it this way. Your feet will not hurt you like they used to, and you can go out and play."

That did bring a small smirk to Puddinhead's face. She stepped tenderly up the walk, feeling how firmly the shoes hugged her feet. She stood on her tiptoes, and then hopped. The pain was becoming a vague memory. Puddinhead looked at her daddy with a mischievous grin, and her daddy knew she would be all right.

Evening Games

The best time of the year for Puddinhead and her sisters was the long summer days that happened in August. The early evening hour was the most enjoyable time for all the houses on Ryan Street. Many of the teens would come out and organize several games where everyone could play. Puddinhead and all her sisters were one of the first families to finish and clean up their dinner so they could join a team. Puddinhead now loved her shoes because her feet did not bother her anymore. Everybody got used to seeing her wearing them, and a few other children down the street had shoes like hers, too.

The parents sat on the porches and talked while the games went on the entire evening.

Puddinhead wanted to play, even though most children her age were still very shy, did not run fast, and chose not to come over. Joey, one of the older boys started calling out the teams. Puddinhead was chosen very quickly because, even though she was the youngest member, she was really tall for five years old and challenged other children who were six and seven. The teams were balanced and set. "Let's play kickball!" The laughter was so contagious and the jokes were so outrageous that the stunts from the evening games would be talked about by everyone for years and years.

One time Leah got nervous and, for some reason, picked up first base when she stopped there. She forgot that she had it in her hand and kept on running to the other bases. Her teammate had to run really fast to catch up with her so he could tag the base. At the same time, the opposite team's first baseman had to run over to her to get the base back. Then Leah started running super fast after she got to home plate because she had to go to the bathroom. She turned to go into the house and saw ten kids chasing her. That was when she realized she still had the base in her hand. Both teams fell down laughing.

Joey's older sister, Ashley kicked the ball like a major league football player. She would kick so hard that the ball seemed to sail through the air forever. The other team members would get ready and set themselves for the longest shot by putting the best catchers and the quickest runners in the outfield. The bases were loaded and the play was in motion.

Ashley came up to kick with the ceremony of greeting the crowds, waving thumbs up, and hand signs of a champ, while pretend announcers stated she was going to kick the ball at least twenty houses away. Puddinhead was on first base, positioned to run all the way around to home plate because she knew there would be enough time.

The ball rolled in a crooked fashion, and that did not satisfy Ashley. She tossed it back to the pitcher. The second pitch was a fast ball and again, Ashley just wasn't ready. Her teammates started shouting, "Ashley, Ashley, Ashley!" The opposite team was gearing up for the super kick. The next ball was shot like a bullet. Ashley made a running start and kicked so hard that the ball broke onto her foot and stayed there.

Everyone was so busy screaming, "Catch the ball!" that they did not hear or see the popped ball flapping on Ashley's foot. Ashley started running around the bases with the ball still stuck on her foot.

The outfielders, confused, started yelling, "Where is the ball?" Ashley scooped up Puddinhead, carrying her along while she ran—and the ball stayed stuck on her right foot. Ashley delivered Puddinhead to home plate, dropping her on the ground. Puddinhead laughed so hard that she did not feel her bottom hurting from the rough landing.

Ashley's team made many distracting moves to cover this up by telling the outfielders they saw the ball roll in the gutter far down the street. It took a moment before the other team members realized what actually happened. Then total pandemonium broke out. Both teams were shouting and arguing about what was fair and not fair. Someone tried to erase the four home runs just won on the scoreboard. Another just took up the bases and proclaimed the game was over. And Ashley kept on running all over the neighborhood, scaring the younger children with the ball on her foot.

Viola!

A new game began; chase, get tagged, and then you are out. Everyone ran and ran and ran until the parents raised their hands, declaring that the evening games were over.

It was time to go inside and go to bed. Daddy told Leah to take her sisters upstairs to wash up and go to bed. Mom, Daddy, and baby Emmanuel, Jr., had their room downstairs, but all the other children had theirs upstairs. Since Leah had to prepare the pajamas and bath water first, Puddinhead tiptoed downstairs into the living room and sat in her favorite red chair. She pressed her head firmly on the back of the chair and soothingly supported her arms on the rests. Closing her eyes she pictured herself running so fast next time that she would even outrun Ashley. Her body tenderly swayed back and forth. The comfort and excitement of the day made a stronger picture in her mind. She would remember it for a long time.

Another memory came to Puddinhead. *What was it Grannie said the last time I went to church with her?* Puddinhead pondered. *Grannie had said, "Miriam, you are very smart. God gave you this brain that can do many things,"* Puddinhead thought. *It was . . . God who made me smart like this. I can run and sing. Also, Leah and Zirah are teaching me how to read their books. I like to do many things. Sometimes my mind is so full of ideas. God, can you hear my brain working? I should say thank you to God for these things. Hello, God. Where are you? Hmmm?*

Leah called from upstairs rushing to get her chores done, "Puddinhead, wait for me! I will be down. We only have a few minutes before bedtime."

The End

listen|imagine|view|experience

AUDIO BOOK DOWNLOAD INCLUDED WITH THIS BOOK!

In your hands you hold a complete digital entertainment package. Besides purchasing the paper version of this book, this book includes a free download of the audio version of this book. Simply use the code listed below when visiting our website. Once downloaded to your computer, you can listen to the book through your computer's speakers, burn it to an audio CD or save the file to your portable music device (such as Apple's popular iPod) and listen on the go!

How to get your free audio book digital download:

1. Visit www.tatepublishing.com and click on the e|LIVE logo on the home page.
2. Enter the following coupon code:
   5c7a-4f79-ac96-45eb-daf5-0be3-4678-4be0
3. Download the audio book from your e|LIVE digital locker and begin enjoying your new digital entertainment package today!